Print Version
Copyright 2021
Carol-Lynn Rössel
All Rights Reserved

For Jenny-Lynn Azarian, Carl Gregory Raymond Rössel & Claire Hersom.

About Monhegan Island
Coordinates: 43*45'44"N 69*19'13"W

MONHEGAN is a plantation in Lincoln County, Maine, U.S.A. including Monhegan Island & nearby Manana Island, which helps form Monhegan Harbor.
It sits in the Gulf of Maine, part of the Atlantic Ocean, about 12 nautical miles from Maine's coast.
Monhegan is 1.75 miles (2,82km) long & .75 of a mile (1.2 kilometers) wide. Of its total area of 4.5 square miles, (12 km2); 0.9 square miles (2.3 km2) is land.
On the Atlantic flyway, it is a stopover for migrating birds.
Monhegan Associates, formed in 1954 by Ted Edison, owns & protects some 350 undeveloped acres, for public access to 20 miles of challenging trails along rocky ledges & to Cathedral Woods, where visitors build fairy houses.
The name Monhegan (Monchiggon) means "out to sea island" in Algonquian.
It was visited by explorers: Samuel de Champlain (1603) Martin Pring (1604), George Weymouth (1614) & Captain John Smith (1614).
Native Americans knew Monhegan to be a prime fishing area. Visiting traders & fishermen taught English to Monhegan sagamore (chief) Samoset. In 1621, he visited the Pilgrim settlers at Plymouth, Massachussetts & greeted them with: "Welcome Englishmen."
Since 1890, Monhegan has lured artists, writers & photographers, many of them summer visitors like Robert Henri, George Bellows, Edward Hopper, Rockwell Kent & Jamie Wyeth, whose cottage is pictured in this book.

Across
the
room
waits
a
wooden

Truck.

A hegehog

stands on its roof

She is round
and plump

and her pinafore
hides a dress
with gingham
checks.

Beside the truck

waits a squad
of ducks.

Their number

always

is

six.

Two sit on the hood.

Two sit in the cab.

And the last
two

sit
in
back.

This moonlight night they're again all packed. Adventure once more they seek.

But they'll never move 'till the lights come on. They won't travel till it's dark.

The lights go on about half past nine. They wait until

it is TEN.

Then they come alive.

they

ride.

When

comes

they
PARK.

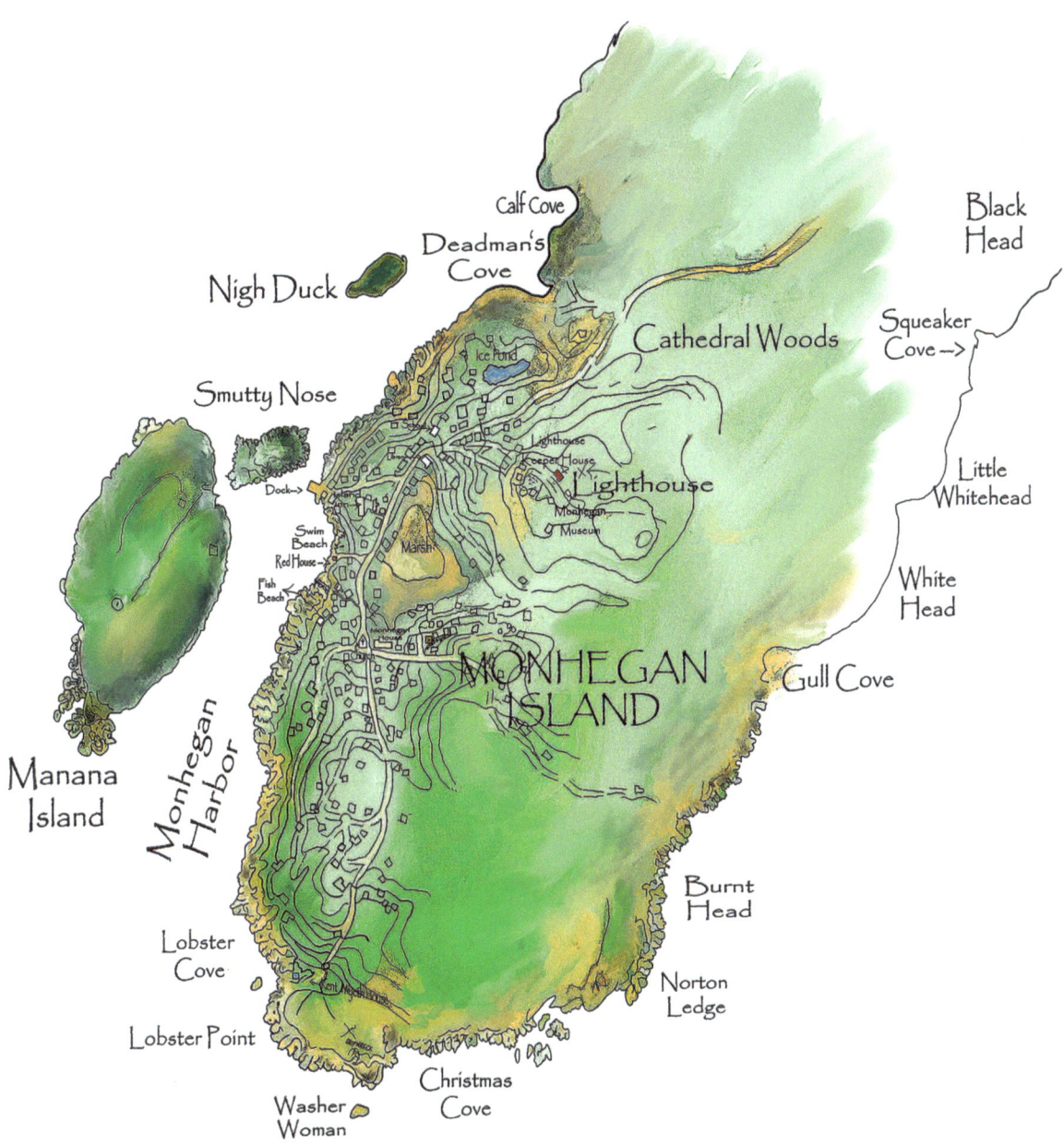

Contact Information

Twitter: @CarolLynnRossel
Facebook: https://facebook.com/carollynn.rossel
Instagram: carollynnrossel
Webpage: carollynnrossel.com

Kent/Wyeth Cottage

About the Author

CAROL-LYNN RÖSSEL loves to visit Monhegan Island, Maine & to take photographs of its places & people. When a girl on Staten Island in New York City, Santa left her, each year, a doll & a book. One year he added a camera, film & her grandmother's painting box. These led her to her life's work.

Carol-Lynn's monochrome photography has been exhibited internationally. Her lovable Teddy Bear designs for collectors & companies have charmed children worldwide. Many of her 25 published books feature dolls & Teddy Bears.

Her house is full of toys, many of which she has made. Some were models for the characters in this book. She took their portraits, combined them with her Monhegan Island photos & used these composites as reference for digitally painted illustrations.

She lives in Central Maine, is learning to play the ukulele & is a member of SCBWI New England.

LEAH HARADEN

MONHEGAN

Where is the

Red

Ukulele?

CPSIA information can be obtained
at www.ICGtesting.com
Printed in the USA
BVHW021237030222
627978BV00007B/471